A Lullaby for Little One

Dawn Casey

Illustrated by Charles Fuge

nosy crow

Down in the woods in the late evening sun,
Big Daddy Rabbit said,

"Come,
Little One!"

"Let's race and let's chase,
and let's laugh and let's leap!

We'll have lots of fun,
then you must go to sleep."

So, they **raced** and they **chased** . . .

. . . and they shouted, "Woo-hoo!"

They whooped and they swooped . . .
and Owl called,
"Twit-tu-woo!"

They played

hide-and-seek . . .

. . . and found Mouse,

"Peek-a-boo!"

They splashed
and they sploshed . . .

. . . and then Bear

joined in, too!

The last of the sun warmed the big happy crew.
They danced and they shouted
and all sang,

"Ya-hoooOOO!"

They whirled and they twirled
with a laugh and a leap . . .

... 'til they tumbled

and rolled in a glorious heap.

But . . .

. . . Little One suddenly whimpered,

"BOO-HOOOOOO!"

And Big Daddy Rabbit said,

"What a to-do!"

"Was that all too much of
a hullaballoo?
I think that it's time for
a lullaballoo."

So Big Rabbit swayed
in the slow-setting sun,
as he hugged and he hummed,

"Hush-a-bye,
Little One."

Baby snuffled
and snuggled.
They both curled up tight.

"I love you, my Little One,
sweet dreams, good night."